THE CAPTAIN'S CABIN

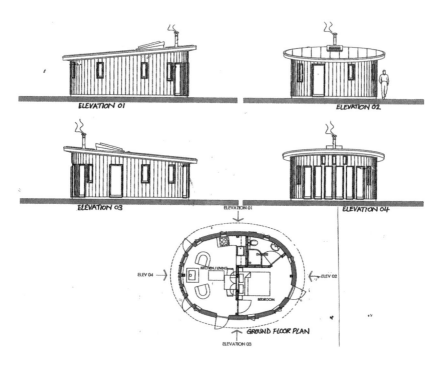

*The Captain's Cabin, Plans and drawings designed by
Architect Roderick James and Amanda Markham*

The
Captain's
Cabin

ALEXANDER McCALL SMITH

Illustrations by
Iain McIntosh

OUT *of the* BLUE

First published in Great Britain in 2022
by Out of the Blue

Out of the Blue
Eagle Rock
Achabeag
Lochaline
Morvern
Argyll
PA80 5XU

9 8 7 6 5 4 3 2 1

www.outoftheblue.uk.com

ISBN 978 1 3999 2020 9

Photography credits: The Captain's Cabin, designed by Architect Roderick James
and Amanda Markham, Plans and drawings, pg ii, © Roderick James; 'Arcadia',
pg ix, from P&O Pencillings, © Pencillings Heritage Collection; The Captain's
Cabin on the Old Chapel, pg3, © Nigel Rigden; Ardtornish House, pg 5,
© Ardtornish Estate; 'Down River' from Pencillings, pg 9, © P&O Heritage
Collection; 'Berenice', pg 30, © Tim Wright; The Sound of Mull,
pg 32, © Nigel Rigden; Saloon chairs from Arcadia in the Captain's; Cabin,
pg 42, © Nigel Rigden; The Saloon in the Captain's Cabin, pg 44, © Nigel
Rigden; Bedroom photo, pg 46, © Nigel Rigden; Cabin & Sundeck,
pg 47, © Nigel Rigden; Mission Hospital at Shyira, Rwanda, pg
52, © Dr N. M. James; Jamie's Farm photography © Lydia Booth Photography

Typeset in Bembo by Edward Crossan
Printed and bound by Gomer Press Limited, Wales

For
Jamie, Jake & Tish
and
All the staff at Jamie's Farm

AUTHOR'S NOTE

The story that follows is partly true and partly imagined. The Captain's Cabin does, in fact, exist, as do some of the characters. As for the Captain himself, and his father, I am not so sure, but if he did not exist, then perhaps he should have. Jamie's Farms do exist, and it is absolutely the case that Roderick and Amanda James drove their car ahead of mine along that road in Morvern not all that long ago.

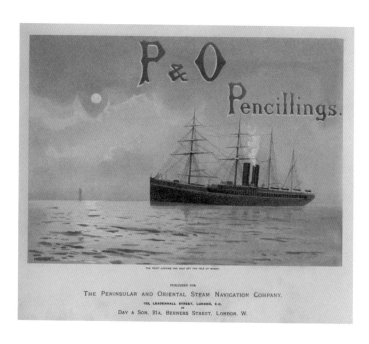

'Arcadia' © *P&O Heritage*

I.

"A shilling life," wrote the poet W.H. Auden, "will give you all the facts …"

It will indeed. A short biography will tell you all you need to know about many people, about where they were born, where they lived, and how they earned their living. For most of us, a few sentences will do all that work, will set out with sufficient clarity the landscape of our life, showing its saliences, its small moments of triumph, its feel, its texture. Others may require slightly more, but, even then, a biography does not have to run to hundreds of pages to do justice to its subject.

So what will a shilling life tell us about the Captain? That he went to sea as a young man, barely out of boyhood? That he served his country at a time of great peril? That he built a house on top of a chapel in a remote part of Scotland? That people said of him, *The Captain was a good man?* That many in Scotland wept when they heard he had died? Facts like that tell us something of a life, but perhaps not quite as much as we might wish to know. Sometimes, we would like to find out a little more – not much, but just enough to imagine that the person in question is still somehow with us, not there, of course, but not entirely absent. And that curiosity on our part speaks to something rather interesting, perhaps – the belief that our world is composed not just of those who are here right now, alive amongst us, but includes those who lived before us and whose voices might still be heard if we listen hard enough.

I had no idea of who the Captain was until that October day when Roderick James and his wife Amanda drove ahead of my car up the winding road that leads from Lochaline to Drimnin. It is a road I know reasonably well. In late spring, it is lined in places with beds of wild garlic and bluebells that scent the air as one goes past – everything grows with boundless enthusiasm in that wet part of Scotland. To the west, just below the road, beyond the rocky shore, the tides of the Sound of Mull separate Morvern from the Isle of Mull only a short distance away. Broad-leafed trees, some new, some ancient, make a high canopy of green; burns trickle or tumble, according to mood, from rising ground that often fades into cloud or veils of rain. It is a liquid landscape, this, of lochs and rivers and moist emptiness. It was here that Somerled held sway in the time of those ancient, half-Irish kingdoms; it was here that James Macpherson would have us believe that Ossian spun sagas of Fingal and other heroes. In the mist that wreathes these hills and shores, one might believe anything – even that there was once a Scottish Homer who kept alive the exploits of these romantic warriors.

I followed their car when it turned off the narrow single-track road to climb up to the place where, years earlier, a simple stone chapel had once served the needs of the people of these parts. The chapel is still there, some time ago converted into a house and still lived in today. But there is another dwelling – a curious, semi-ovoid structure built on top of the old chapel and reached by a modern external stair. This is the Captain's Cabin, and this was what Roderick and Amanda wanted to show me.

The Captain's Cabin on the Old Chapel

They unlocked the door and admitted me to the cabin, and all at once I had that impression that you occasionally get in a building – the feeling that this is the home of somebody who has just stepped out of the room, who is not long away.

I looked out over the view to the front. Across the sound, Tobermory could just be made out on its distant hillside. A lone boat ploughed its course across a field of blue, leaving a white trail, a line behind it that faded quickly. A couple of gulls dipped and swerved across the sky, mewing in the wind.

I asked Roderick whether he could tell me something about the Captain, and he replied that he knew only a few facts, and that he was not even sure that those were correct. It would be good, he said, to find out more, though, because people who came to stay in the Captain's Cabin might be interested in learning something about him. I knew, then, that I would have to satisfy my curiosity and find out more about the man whose life and personality were on show in the artefacts this room contained, in the furniture, and in the pictures lining its walls.

So began my enquiry. And here, in the few pages that follow, is what I have been able to find out about Captain Thomas Fitzroy Douglas, who lived in this cabin not all that long ago and whose few possessions remain there, the remnants of a life spent more at sea than on land: a sextant, a couple of salvaged chairs, pictures of the ships that took him on his travels or of the yachts he sailed in the waters round Mull and its nearby islands.

Non omnis moriar, proclaimed Horace. I shall not entirely die. He was right: we leave things behind; we leave traces of our lives; we are remembered in incidental and unexpected ways; something of us always remains. Few people talk about the Captain today, but you might care to spend a few moments now in the company of this man who has given his name to a rather beautiful and unusual dwelling in a quiet corner of Scotland. This is what I discovered.

There was one principal source, and this came to my attention more or less by accident. Roderick telephoned me one day in a state of some excitement. He had just heard from Hugh Raven, a member of the family who had lived on Ardtornish Estate for over ninety years, that a trunk of papers had been found in a dusty corner of one of the attics in Ardtornish House. Nobody knew how the trunk came to be there, although on it there was pasted a handwritten note asking that the contents be looked after "until I get back". No name was given, but when Hugh investigated the contents of the trunk he discovered that the diaries it contained were those of both Captain Thomas Fitzroy Douglas and his father, Captain Andrew McNair Douglas. There were, in addition, several small notebooks of poems, many written in pencil. These notebooks bore the name of Thomas, the son, rather than Andrew, the father.

Knowing of his interest in the Douglas family, Hugh had passed the entire contents on to Roderick. "These old diaries could be interesting," he said. "One day somebody might care to go through them."

Ardtornish House

Artefacts in the Captain's Cabin

I was to be that person, and what follows is the result of my reading over several days of the meticulous recording, by two members of the Douglas family, of the daily course of their lives. The story that emerged is one of two generations rather than one. I had thought that I would write the story of one captain, but it ended up being the story of two. Each of us thinks our individual history begins with our birth, our entry to this world; it does not. We are more than one person. What happens to us starts with those who precede us, with our grandparents, and with their parents. What we think is the first chapter of the story is often only the mid-point of a tale that began a long time earlier than we imagine.

The Captain's father was a sailor too. Captain Andrew McNair Douglas was the very picture of a nineteenth century merchant navy captain – weather-beaten and whiskered, with the clear eyes of one accustomed to staring into long distances. He was born in Dumfries in 1853, at the height of the reign of that unsmiling matriarch, Victoria, whose navies and armies bestrode half the world. Andrew Douglas left school at the age of seventeen to go to sea as a junior officer on the *Cutty Sark*, the

famous clipper that brought tea from India to Britain via the Cape of Good Hope. He served on the vessel's maiden voyage to Shanghai, sailing under Captain Moodie, a cousin of his father's. He remained on the ship for some years, and was still on her when she started to carry wool from Australia.

Cutty Sark

The arrival of steamships, though, was unsettling for those who still sailed under canvas, and Andrew decided to accept an offer of a job with a firm of tea importers in London. Transporting tea from China had given Andrew a taste for it, and he had discovered that his discriminating palate enabled him to identify subtle nuances in flavour. He did well in this firm, and might have risen to the top of the industry had he stayed the course. But the lure of the sea was too great, and he returned to the merchant navy, eventually becoming captain of the *Arcadia*, a passenger ship built by Harland and Wolf in Belfast in 1888 for use on voyages between Britain and India. This ship can be seen in a photograph, taken by the Captain himself, that still hangs on the wall of his cabin. She was a handsome vessel, capable of carrying 250 first-class passengers, 171 second-class, and a crew of 238. Also in the cabin you may find a book, *Pencillings*, containing sketches by W.W. Lloyd, an artist who travelled to India on the Arcadia and recorded his impression in witty pencil portraits and cartoons.

Arcadia's role was to carry the mail between India and Britain as well as providing passenger services. The journey took over three weeks, with the ship calling at Gibralter, Marseilles, Port Said, and Aden before arriving in Bombay. All through this lengthy journey the ship's captain presided over every aspect of the lives of those on board, passengers and crew alike. Although ships' captains did not have the power to conduct wedding ceremonies – that was always a popular myth – in this case Captain Douglas, being a Justice of the Peace, believed, wrongly, that he was entitled to conduct such ceremonies at sea. He was cautious about shipboard romances and before he married passengers he always insisted on evidence that the couple had known one another before they came on board. He applied this rule strictly, after he had been obliged to separate one couple who had decided on marrying at the beginning of the voyage and who had fallen out with one another by the time they docked in Aden. A more melancholy duty confronted him when a passenger succumbed to illness and had to be buried at sea. He always found the words *we therefore commit his body to the deep* hard to say without a trembling of his voice, and as captain he could not let his emotions show. Similarly, at Sunday services, when together with the passengers assembled on deck he joined in the singing of *For those in peril on the sea*, he was careful to make sure that he maintained a calm composure. It would not do for the passengers to think that the choice of hymn referred in any way to their own position. Indeed, the company had suggested that this hymn be replaced with something less concerning, but Captain Douglas had firmly resisted any change. "It is important," he pointed out, "to acknowledge, as this hymn does, that the Almighty does, in fact, *bid the mighty ocean deep, its own appointed limits keep*. It is reassuring, surely, for those who are nervous sailors to be made aware of that protection."

'Down River' from Pencillings © *P&O Heritage*

The passengers came from all walks of life. Those were the days of the British Raj, and an endless stream of officials, engineers, and commercial people was needed to run the inflated imperial project. But there were others whose purpose was a more personal one. These included children who were carried back from India, uprooted from life with their parents, to be sent off to school in a cold and distant island, unhappy exiles from a sunny childhood of warmth and freedom. Empires involve sacrifice just as they involve exploitation. Normal family life may be impossible, or at least severely constrained by duty and distance. Hardship and illness were never far away. Visit the cemeteries of the hill stations and administrative centres, and reflect on the story spelled out on the gravestones; look at the age of those who are interred there; read the terse biographies that the graves narrate, the stories of lonely lives cut short by malaria, by snake bite, by typhoid and cholera, or by violence – because not everyone passively accepted the authority of those set in authority over them.

Children, soldiers, civil servants: these all appeared in the passenger lists that were placed before Captain Douglas by the purser before the ship set sail. There were others, though, who featured regularly on these lists – these were the members of the so-called fishing fleet, the young women who went out to India with the specific purpose of finding a husband. One of these was Molly Pybus, the daughter of a prosperous Sussex farmer. Molly booked her passage on the *Arcadia* in 1893. Because the purser came from Lewes, and because she was travelling on a first-class ticket, he decided to seat her at the Captain's Table. He needed an extra single woman to ensure that thirteen did not sit down to dinner, and so Molly found herself as one of the guests who were privileged to sit with Captain Douglas in the principal dining room, to the annoyance of virtually all other passengers who were not so favoured, and who thought that they, as much as anybody deserved the honour.

To be a member of the fishing fleet was by no means the first choice of every young woman who embarked on a mail steamer to India. Most of the fleet's members, in fact, chose to try their luck in India only for want of any better opportunity to find a suitable young man at home. Life was harsh in a society where the options for women were limited: there were relatively few careers that were open to women, and the pressure to marry was intense. Somebody in her late twenties, or even less, might be considered to be on the shelf by the standards of the time, and competition for husbands was fierce. But there would always be a not-too-fussy captain in the Indian Army or an administrator in an obscure corner of a distant state who would be looking for a wife and was ready for the plucking. These young women flocked to India, usually not knowing anything about life there, but determined to take this last chance to find a lonely young man, starved of female company, and therefore only too eager to meet them.

On arrival in India, members of the fishing fleet would normally stay with parental friends or contacts who were aware of the expectation that they would launch their charge into society. Social fixtures would have been planned well in advance of the arrival of the candidates, and results awaited with trepidation. An attractive young woman would be in great demand at parties and dances at the local club, and the most eligible of the fleet would quickly be snapped up. Some young women found themselves at parties on the evening of arrival, or at least within a day of two of their disembarking, and in some cases engagements, and marriage, would follow within little more than a few weeks. Then came the dawning of reality, as the new wife accompanied her husband back from his leave to his station in some remote part of the sprawling Raj, to a life in an isolated bungalow, attended by servants, but deprived, sometimes for months on end, of company to whom she could talk. Better-starred marriages, of course, were made, and life might be anything but lonely for those who found husbands posted to the major towns and cities. Life in Calcutta, for example, would hardly be dull for a couple who enjoyed tennis or bridge or any of the other diversions available in those places. And then there was the summer, when people of necessity decamped to the hill stations, to places like Ooty or Simla, where the social whirl was non-stop.

Molly Pybus was the oldest of three sisters. Two had married before they were twenty-two: one to a lawyer, and another to a housemaster at a boys' boarding school. That left Molly, who, at twenty-six was thought to be in real danger of ending up a permanent spinster. A letter was written to her mother's sister, who was married to the manager of a bank in Bombay and had offered in the past to act as hostess to any of her nieces who might like to visit India "for social reasons", as she delicately put it.

Molly was not unattractive and there had been no shortage of admirers. None of them, though, had seemed to meet her high standards, and her mother privately despaired that they ever would. Perhaps India would be different. "You really must make an effort," her mother said to her. "Every man has his drawbacks – even Daddy, with his … well, you know what I'm referring to. One simply has to compromise. That's what life is about you know: constant compromise."

Molly had no interest in India. She had heard that you could very easily become ill there – indeed she knew, personally, of two people who had gone there and died within weeks. Another, the cousin of a school friend, had ended up running away from her husband and being lost for several days in the jungle. It was a miracle, people said, that she had survived. And Molly had an additional concern – that she would fail to find a husband in the time allocated her and that she would be one of those who were sent back home, returned empty, as the cruel expression went.

In the face of intense pressure from her mother, Molly agreed to go, and found herself in due course on the *Arcadia*, lying on the bunk in her first-class cabin, listening to the throb of the ship's engine somewhere down below, wondering how hot the weather might become and whether her nose would bleed, as it sometime did on warm days at home. She had not gone in for dinner on that first night at sea: sea-sickness was a perfectly good excuse in the first days of the voyage, although Molly was not affected. She was suffering, rather, from pangs of doubt about what awaited her at her destination. She did not want to be in Bombay. She did not want to spend every evening at the club, dancing with eager young men. And they would be eager, she thought, because Molly was only too well aware of how attractive men found her. That was the problem. They became too attentive, and that put her off. She did not want to be landed with a gushing young man who would paw her at every opportunity and converse about nothing but hunting or polo or whatever it was that such young men talked about. She wanted a more mature man – a man who would be content with his own company and who would let her get on with the pursuits she enjoyed, which included philately, embroidery, going for walks with dogs, and painting with watercolour paints. A mature man would understand all that and not interfere with any of it. That's what she wanted, she decided: a man who knew his place and would stick to it. *Somebody about forty*, she thought.

That, as it happened, was the exact age of Captain Andrew McNair Douglas. He had celebrated his fortieth birthday in the early days of the voyage, just as the *Arcadia* entered the troubled waters of the Bay of Biscay. And he had found his gaze falling repeatedly and, he hoped, not too noticeably, on the attractive young woman the purser had seated at his table.

"Would you mind passing me the salt?" was the first thing he had said to her.

And she, with a quite charming smile, had done as he asked.

"Salt does add something," she remarked as she passed him the heavy nickel-silver salt cellar.

"It certainly does," he agreed, and thought, at that moment, that he must marry her, and that he should make sure that all arrangements were in place before they reached Bombay and the waiting ranks of eligible young men.

But when, and how, might the Captain declare himself? There was no point in wasting time. Already there were signs of shipboard romances among the other passengers, and the Captain had noticed several young men lurking around that spot on the deck where Molly liked to sit in a deck chair and read. Understanding their motives, the Captain was able to instruct his deck hands discreetly but pointedly to concentrate their deck-scrubbing activities in the immediate vicinity of these potential suitors, splashing them with as much water from their buckets as would be possible without raising excessive suspicions. That worked well enough during the day, but it still left long evenings during which potential competition needed to be seen off. This meant that the Captain became a regular at every event attended by Molly, including dances, evenings in which the newly-invented game of bridge was played, and fancy dress competitions. At the dances he impressed Molly with his nimble footwork, the result of a background of climbing rigging on the *Cutty Sark*; on the bridge evenings he excelled through his ability to remember which cards had gone out and to anticipate which were likely to be in opposition hands; and in the fancy-dress competitions he simply went as a Ship's Captain and was regularly chosen as a winner by the purser, whose job it was to do the judging.

He need not have made the effort. Molly had already fallen in love with the Captain and when he eventually proposed, twelve days into the voyage, she accepted him rapidly, and with some relief. To become engaged to the captain of the very ship on which the fishing fleet set out to sail, struck her as being the best conceivable solution to what she had come to think of as "the husband problem". Now that marriage was out of the way, she could get down to the business of leading her life as she wanted to lead it.

"I think we should marry immediately," said the Captain on the morning after their engagement. "I believe I have the authority, as captain of this ship, to perform a marriage ceremony."

"Are you sure about that?" asked Molly.

"Reasonably sure," replied the Captain. "I have on occasion officiated at a marriage ceremony on board, and nobody has complained so far."

The purser was not so sanguine in his views. "Some may speculate," he pointed out, "that it is unusual to marry oneself, so to speak – not that I'm questioning your view of the situation, Captain. I have complete confidence in your judgement on all matters."

"Good," said the Captain. "In that case, we shall have the ceremony tomorrow. You and the Ship's Engineer may be witnesses."

"You'll need to change the wording slightly," suggested the purser. "You'll have to say, *Do I take thee as my lawful wedded wife?*"

"That will easily be done," said the Captain.

Molly was perfectly happy with the proposed arrangements. The Captain was a fine-looking man. He was kind and considerate. He was forty – which was what she wanted – and she was completely confident that she would be happy. In that respect, she was to be proved right. She and the Captain complemented one another ideally.

"Bless you, my dear," said the Captain. "Bless you for coming into my life."

"I feel that way too," said Molly.

"You are very fortunate to have found such a man as the

Captain," the purser whispered to Molly. "You could have done far worse – there's no doubt that at all." And here he cast a glance in the direction of the ship's engineer, with his oil-stained countenance, his dirty fingernails, and his colourful way of putting things.

They boarded the *Arcadia* bachelor and spinster; they went ashore in Bombay husband and wife. In the company offices there, under the suspicious eye of the Parsi head-clerk, the Captain introduced his new wife to the local manager and made his request for matrimonial leave. It was potentially an awkward request, in the view of the Parsi clerk an outrageous one: a captain cannot normally leave his vessel just as it arrives in a foreign port and is preparing to embark passengers for the return voyage. The *Arcadia's* first officer, however, was as keen to prove himself as the company was to try him out, and he readily volunteered to assume command of the ship. The company had another mail steamer undergoing repairs in Bombay and this would be ready to leave for the voyage home in less than a month's time. The man designated to skipper that ship had been ill with a severe bout of malaria, coupled with a gastric ulcer, and ideally would need several months of recuperation before resuming duties. The Captain could assume command of that ship and then be reunited in Southampton with the *Arcadia* for its next voyage out to India.

They lost no time in heading for Simla. It was just the right time to make the journey, as the summer season was about to begin and those who could travel to the hill stations were already boarding the trains that would take them from the unbearable heat of the plains. The Captain was used to the sights and sounds of India, but for Molly it was all new and quite overwhelming. Gazing out of the train window as they made its way up to Chandigarh, she reflected with relief on the escape she had been vouchsafed. Had she done what had been expected of her, had she married the first dim district officer to propose to her, some *pukka sahib* practitioner of polo and pig-sticking, this could so easily have been the world in which she could find herself – this landscape of aimless tracks, of arid scrub, of stony hills. And for all the colour and romance of this country, there was also so much noise and pushing and sheer need: the heaving seas of travellers who crowded the railway stations; the holy mendicants with their clouded, unseeing eyes; the thin, ubiquitous children; the arrogant cattle wandering untouched through the bustling streets. She closed her eyes and imagined the gentle hills around their farm in Sussex; the neat hedgerows, the geese about the pond in the farmyard, the narrow lanes along which only the occasional cart went by, the silences and the birdsong that broke them.

The Captain was unused to having time on his hands and for the first few days in Simla he was restless. There was company to be had in the club, but the men to whom he talked there all belonged to a world very different from his own. He wanted to talk about the sea, but they had nothing to say about that.

"The sea's very much the same wherever you look," one of them remarked. "Quite frankly, one bit of sea is much the same as any other."

The Captain looked at him with incomprehension bordering on pity. He thought that about the land. The sea was in constant movement; the land was always there, always the same.

For Molly, there were tea parties and an embroidery circle. And there were letters home to be written – one every other day, consigned by bearer to the local post office from which they were sent on what seemed to her to be an impossibly long journey back to Sussex. Her mother replied, giving her news of her sisters, each of whom now had a young child. She wondered when that would happen to her. The thought frightened her. She was scared of the prospect of childbirth and preferred not to think about it.

One of the matrons who presided over regular tea parties, the wife of a man in the army of officials making up the Viceroy's entourage, took her aside and spoke reassuringly of the "great adventure" that lay before her. "It will be over before you know it," she said. "And there he'll be, in your arms, filling his lungs with air." She paused, and then added, "It's our higher duty, you know."

The Captain said to her one morning, "I don't really like it here, you know. I don't like these people very much. Oh, some of them are all right, I suppose, in their way. But when I have them on board my ship it's different. I'm the captain and they defer to me. But here, they strut around so self-importantly."

She knew what he meant. If anything, the women were worse, seeming to be more aware of rank and distinction than the men.

"I want to go home," she said.

"We shall," he said. "In a couple of weeks we can go back down to Bombay. The ship will be ready."

She counted the days. Five days before they were due to depart, she was stung by a scorpion. Her lower leg began to swell and an angry red circle developed around the site of the sting. A doctor came, and then a nurse, brisk and efficient. A lotion was dabbed on her skin and it provided some relief, but the swelling seemed only to get worse. She thought, "I shall die here, just like so many of them die. They come to this country and they die."

"You're not going to die," said the nurse. "Plenty of people die, but I don't think you're going to be one of them."

The swelling subsided. She went for a walk with the Captain and they stopped to pick wildflowers. He named the flowers, giving each a Latin name. She complimented him on his knowledge of botany.

"I can never remember which plant is which," she said.

"I'm making the names up," he said, smiling art her. "I have no idea what these flowers are called. The really important thing is that they are beautiful."

She looked at him. She felt rather surprised that she had married a man who could say something like that. There were so few men who would say such a thing, and she had somehow found one of them. She reached for his hand. He seemed surprised, but he was pleased, and he said, "My dear," just that – nothing more. Love was a strange thing, she thought. It came upon you almost like a chill, something you caught from somewhere. You could shrug it off – just as you could shrug off an incipient cold – but if that did not happen, then it became something else, something much deeper and more significant, and you realised that it had somehow changed you inside, changed the person that you were.

In June 1900 Molly gave birth to a son. This was Thomas Fitzroy Douglas, who was born while his father was at sea. They were living then in a cottage on the family farm in Sussex, but the Captain was keen to move them back to Scotland, where he had inherited a house in Broughty Ferry, just outside Dundee. Molly was uncertain: Scotland seemed so far away, so different from what she was used to, but she could see that her husband's heart was set on the move, and she assented.

The house in Broughty Ferry had belonged to the Captain's aunt. She was a doctor's widow and had been childless. The Captain, being her nearest relative, inherited not only the house, but all its contents and a sizeable amount of money squirrelled away in an interest-bearing British Linen Bank account. The furniture was not to Molly's taste, nor were the paintings that adorned the walls. These were scenes of heather-covered hillsides, of Highland cattle wading through burns or standing, self-consciously by the edge of lochs – a shortbread-tin vision of a Scotland that almost existed, but not quite. Molly preferred the paintings the Captain had acquired over the years – the full-rigged ships, pennants flying; the men-of-war locked in explosive battle with the French, puffs of smoke emanating from their gun ports. Why did men have to fight, she wondered. They were like stags in the rutting season, horns locked, bellowing out their challenge – fighting over *us*, she thought.

At an early age – he was just seven – Thomas was sent away to a small boarding school near Perth. It was not Molly's decision – she was opposed to the idea that children should be sent away for their schooling, but the Captain was insistent. "If we have a daughter next, she can stay at home," he said. "But this is what I want for my son. It will toughen him up."

She wanted to say, "He doesn't need that," but she did not. The Captain was a considerate husband and was not one to insist on getting his way, but on this issue she detected a resolution that she felt she would be unable to shift. She conceded, weeping inconsolably after she had handed Thomas over to the school, under the stern gaze of a forbidding-looking matron. He had clung to her, and she had been obliged to prise his small fingers from her wrist and forearm. There was such strength in his grip – it took her aback; as if he were a drowning child clutching at a life-raft or piece of flotsam.

He learned very little at that school, other than the rules of rugby, the names of the ancient kings of Scotland, and a slew of facts about the great mountains of the world. Mountains were the obsession of his form teacher, a man in his early thirties who had climbed

Willem van de Velde the Younger,
A Dutch man-of-war

the Matterhorn and was notching up every one of Scotland's peaks above three thousand feet. He talked endlessly about mountaineering, using a wheezing projector to show the boys pictures of the summits he had reached, with diagrams of the routes he had followed. They learned the vocabulary of his mystery – cols, spurs, ridges and so on; they learned about the Himalayas and the Andes, about glaciers and volcanoes. *I will lift up mine eyes to the hills,* he wrote

Mr Stuart's skis

in chalk, in large letters, on the blackboard. "Commit that to memory, boys," he said. They did, but wondered why they should remember it.

He was called Mr Stuart. Nobody seemed to know his first name. The boys called him *Ben*, the Gaelic word for mountain. He became Ben Stuart, in the same way as Ben Nevis was Ben Nevis.

One morning, at the assembly called each day after breakfast, the Headmaster announced, "I am very sorry, boys, to tell you that Mr Stuart will not be returning to the school."

The pictures of mountains were removed from the wall. No further mention was made of the Matterhorn, or Mont Blanc, or Buachaille Etive Mòr. There were whispered suggestions; rumours that proliferated and were embellished with each iteration. Mr Stuart had fallen over a cliff. Mr Stuart had broken his ankle and had perished in a snowdrift. Mr Stuart had been swept away by a torrent. A dislodged rock had split Mr Stuart's head and his brain had fallen out, rolling all the way downhill.

Thomas saw Mr Stuart's possessions being loaded into a car. There were several pairs of climbing boots, ice-axes, a leather

Mr Stuart's projector

map-case, his projector. He asked the local minister, who served as the school's chaplain, what had happened to the teacher.

"He has been called to higher things," said the minister.

Thomas learned about impermanence. Up to that point, everything had been fixed and forever. Now he discovered that things might not last – that friendships might come to an end; that what we had we might only have for a short time; that people went away; that the adult world had its secrets and its mysteries; and that not every question you asked received the answer it deserved.

At the age of twelve he went to a larger school, every bit as strange, in its way, as his first, although distinguished for the fear that lay at the heart of its governance. Bullying was rife, and unacted upon by the authorities – endorsed, even, in the name of tradition. Cruel rituals marked entry into each stage of the school's hierarchy, and a code of silence, every bit as strict, it seemed, as Sicilian *omertà* ensured that ill treatment was never reported. Thomas was no unhappier than any of the other boys, but that still meant that he dreaded the beginning of each term and counted the days until its end, as a prisoner might record the passage of his durance with marks scratched on the wall of his cell.

In spite of this, glimmers of light relieved the darkness. There was a music teacher who staged operettas, casting unlikely boys in unlikely roles – to the amusement of all. There was a chemistry teacher who loved mixing home-made explosives. And then there was Mr J.M.C. Robinson, a teacher of English, who introduced Thomas to poetry.

"Never read poetry without speaking it in your head," he said. "Poetry is meant to be spoken."

Mr J.M.C. Robinson singled Thomas out. "I can tell that you have an ear for language," he said. "You can always tell. Some people have it – others don't. I can tell that you are one who does."

Thomas looked down at the floor. He was not sure how to respond. But it was true, he thought: he did like poetry. He loved it.

"So let me read you something," the teacher went on. "There's a poet called Matthew Arnold. I think I mentioned him in class. Do you remember?"

"Yes. I remember."

"He wrote an extraordinary poem. It's called *On Dover Beach*. I'll read it to you, if I may. Would you like me to?"

"Yes. I would. Thank you, Sir."

Mr J.M.C. Robinson closed his eyes. Thomas watched him. Mr J.M.C. Robinson was sixty, somebody had said. Perhaps he would be called to higher things soon.

"It starts like this," said the teacher. "The sea is calm tonight./ The tide is full, the moon lies fair./ Upon the straits; on the French coast, The light/ Gleams and is gone; the cliffs of England stand/ Glimmering and vast ..."

He broke off. "You see what the poet is doing?"

He was not sure.

"He's setting the scene. He's putting us right there, on the beach, standing beside him. We can hear his voice, can't we?"

"I think we can."

"And he's inviting us to look at the sea and share his thoughts about it."

"About the sea?"

"Yes," said Mr J.M.C. Robinson. "About the sea, but also about what the sea represents. Many things are not just the things they are, so to speak; they are something else as well. They are also the things that they *suggest*. That's what metaphor is all about."

"Oh."

"Metaphors are everywhere in our language," Mr J.M.C. Robinson continued. "We become so used to them that we forget that they are metaphors. And the sea, of course, is often used in metaphor. We plumb the depths of an issue, for example. That comes from dropping lead on a bit of line to see what depth the sea is. And they'd have a piece of tallow on the lead so that it could pick up a sample of what lies below. Shell, for instance, or sand. A bit of that would stick to the tallow and come up with the lead."

Thomas was thinking. He did not care about metaphor. But he did like that poem that Mr J.M.C. Robinson finished reciting now. "Are there other poems about the sea?"

"I'm not sure that this one is really about the sea," said Mr J.M.C. Robinson. "It's about the loss of certainty – the loss of things we used to believe in."

"What about Rupert Brooke?"

"Oh, he's the latest thing," said Mr J.M.C. Robinson. "Of course, poets come and go. I'm not sure that Rupert Brooke will stay with us forever."

"There's *Grantchester*. I like that one. Surely people will go on reading that."

"Yes, I suppose so. I have a feeling, though, that Rupert Brooke is going to die. There's something about him that makes me think that. Of course, with this terrible war …"

"Why is it terrible?"

"Because it is. Because it's terrible that young men are shooting one another. Because it's terrible that old men are getting these young men to fight. Because it's terrible that even as we sit here and talk like this, there are countless young men who are enduring every sort of privation on the battlefields. Shivering in the cold. Being soaked and not being able to get dry. Enduring infestation with lice. Sleeping alongside the bodies of their comrades, not knowing that the man beside them is dead, and not just sleeping."

"And Mr Brooke may die?

"It's a feeling I have. He's a bit like Byron, you see. Byron died young."

"We all die, I think." He did not mean to sound disrespectful, but he thought that was how he sounded, anyway.

Mr J.M.C. Robinson had not taken the comment to heart. "Oh, I assure you, I would never aspire to immortality, which may prove to be a curse, after all. Certainly, that was what it was to Sisyphus. And Tantalus, too, poor fellow. Leaving the stage at the right time is the most that we should hope for. Neither too early, nor too late – if you see what I mean."

He did not expect the boy to understand, but there was something about this boy that was different, that suggested that he might grasp these things that would normally be beyond the young. It could be, he thought, that this boy might be one to write poetry. It was possible, he thought; it was just possible. The gods touched a brow at random, and poetry was the result. It could happen even in a place like this, this warren of cold corridors and hearty athletes. It could happen.

"Let's look at *Dover Beach* again," he said. "It's a very sad poem, I think. A grave poem."

He read on, and watched the boy's expression as he uttered the lines. *I'm right,* he thought. *He understands.*

"I'm sick with relief," said Molly to a friend. "If one can be sick with relief, that is. Anyway, you know what I mean."

Her friend nodded. "It could have been so different. I suppose he would have joined up when he left school – if it hadn't been over, that is."

"Yes," Molly said. "He spoke about it as if it was going to be something he would do automatically, like getting a job. He was very matter-of-fact. He said, 'When I leave school, I'll be eighteen, and I suppose I'll go to France.' Those were his words. And then, at the last minute, the whole horrible thing grinds to a halt; the guns fall silent – just in time."

"And yet, all those other mothers …"

Her friend did not have to finish the sentence. The newspaper columns had told that story time and time again, with their dreadful lists, so terse and yet so eloquent.

He went home, but only for a month or so. The Captain had arranged an interview for him with a shipping company that was planning to take on cadets. He would be trained as a mariner, which is what he had announced he wanted to be.

He did well at the interview. One of the members of the panel knew the Captain and just smiled all the way through the encounter, asking no questions of him. Afterwards, they drew him aside and told him that he could start the following week. He would spend a few months on board one of their vessels and then be sent to a maritime college. He would be paid enough to live on and be given a uniform allowance. He would be on trial for three months, but they were sure he would fit the bill.

"The sea is not for everyone," said his father's friend after the interview, "but in your case, I suspect it's in your blood. I think that helps."

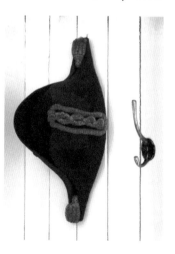

The Captain's naval hat

His father took him to a naval tailor in Glasgow to have him fitted for a uniform. Molly cried when she saw him come back to Broughty Ferry in his new outfit. He asked her why she was crying, and she just shook her head and told him that it was complicated. Mothers, he told himself, are apt to cry for no reason.

"Remember what that uniform stands for," said his father.

Thomas stopped to think, and something that Mr J.M.C. Robinson had said came back to him. "It's a metaphor," he said.

The Captain looked at his son with incomprehension. "It means that you should never do anything low or underhand. It means that you should keep your temper and be fair to all those under your command. It means that you should never look down on a man because he doesn't have your education. It means all that."

"I know."

"Good."

He went to sea. On his first voyage a man went overboard off the coast of Ireland. Thomas saw the man slip and fall; one moment he was there, lying on the heaving deck; the next he was gone. He threw a life ring over the side and raised the alarm. When they lowered the boat that went to the man's rescue he found himself in charge, shouting out orders to the men at the oars. Miraculously, they did what he told them to do.

Scrimshaw

"You handled that exactly as you should," said his captain. "We could have lost that man were it not for you."

The man thanked him effusively

from his bunk in the sick bay. He was a deck-hand with only four months to serve before his retirement. He gave Thomas a piece of scrimshaw on which a clipper had been carved. He wanted him to have it, he said, because he had saved his life.

He was keeping a regular diary now, a habit he had started at school. In the entry for that day he wrote, "I did not really think about what I was doing. It happened very quickly. They always say that things happen quickly at sea – it's true. Before you know it, it's happened and the ship has moved on. There's no time to think."

Molly became ill. The Captain got in touch with him and told him he should come home to see her. He arrived just in time – the course of her illness was swift and sudden. Afterwards, the Captain seemed to lose his joy in life. He had largely retired after the scrapping of the *Arcadia*, which took place in 1915, although he continued to do the occasional voyage when the company needed him. He had been a constant smoker, and not long after Molly's death he developed a hacking and persistent cough. Thomas knew what this meant. He sat by his father's bed and read him to him from Frederick Marryat. He loved *Mr Midshipman Easy*, and could listen to it again and again. It was while Thomas was reading this book to him that his breathing stopped. Thomas closed the book and put it down on the bedside table. He was on his own now. He had become the Captain.

He sat down at his father's desk and wrote down some lines that had been going through his head. *You held me as a boy up in the air; / You let me fall, but caught me, / As we shall catch one another/ When it is our turn to fall ...*

Thomas, now the Captain, married at thirty-six, after completing a nine-month voyage that took in South America and the Far East. Taking a long leave of four months, he booked in as a weekly boarder in a hotel in Oban. This hotel was owned by a woman called Elsie McGibbon, who was to become his wife. She was a few years younger than the Captain and had inherited the hotel from her uncle. She persuaded the Captain to resign from the shipping company for which he was then working, and to help her run the hotel. As an inducement, she bought him a half share in a fishing boat called *Lorne Star*. This would give him the chance to go to sea, but not for more than a few days at a time. 'There's no point in having a husband if he's gone for months on end," said Elsie. "No point, as far as I can see."

The Captain did not argue. He enjoyed the short trips that he and his co-owner made to the fishing grounds in the Sea of the Hebrides. They took herring and, in the summer months, mackerel – in great, glistening mounds. He was happiest when at sea, but the days in between, when he and Elsie were in Oban together, were ones of contentment. They hoped for children, but none came. "It doesn't matter," said the Captain. "Our life is otherwise full."

He bought a classic yacht, *Berenice*, from somebody he knew who had sailed it on the Clyde, and he spent long days restoring it. The deck had to be painstakingly re-caulked; the hull scraped back and revarnished; the rigging needed to be replaced. Slowly the boat became sleek again and drew admiring glances from other yachtsmen.

Then came the announcement on the radio. The war they had been talking about in the newspapers had begun. It was as simple as that: a declaration, a few words on the radio, and the whole process started once again.

He said to Elsie, "I shall have to go."

'Berenice'

She looked at him. "But they need you. They still need fish."

He shook his head. "I have to."

She turned away. "Then I'm going to go too."

He pointed out that they were not asking women to go just yet.

"They are," she said. "I did a year's nursing. It was a long time ago, but you don't forget these things. They need nurses."

"And the hotel?"

"Mr Duncan can run that." He was the barman, but he knew all about the running of the business. "He'll keep it going until all this is over."

He tried to think of reasons why she should stay, but none came to mind. "Be very careful," she said.

"*You* be careful," came her reply. "I take it you'll want to be in the navy. The Royal Navy this time, not the merchant navy."

"Yes," he said. "They'll want me there, I think."

She looked at him and smiled. "We never thought this would happen," she said.

"That there would be a war? That we would both go off?'

"Yes."

He was silent. The world was not what he wanted it to be. He wanted it to be a place of peace and harmony. It was anything but. It was a place of anger and confrontation, it seemed.

"I wish I didn't feel like crying," she said. "I wish I were one of these people who was all optimistic and cheerful, saying it will all be over with a few months."

"Unlikely," he said. He had been in Hamburg eighteen months earlier. He had witnessed a march in the street. He had seen the looks on the faces of the men who had set about a man who had attempted to remonstrate with the marchers. He had been shouting out, his voice muffled in pain, *"Ich bin Deutsch!"* but they had paid no heed and he had been pushed to the ground. A young man stepped on his throat, and kept his foot there until he was moved along by one of the other marchers. He had helped the man to his feet. He said, "I am Jewish, you see".

He looked at the retreating marchers, flushed with their tiny, cruel triumph. You did not attempt to reason with people like that.

The Navy, not surprisingly, was pleased to see him. It had found itself enlisting people who had never been to sea, giving them a few short weeks of training, and dispatching them to their ships. Here, by contrast, was a qualified mariner, with wide experience, who could more or less immediately be entrusted with a command. Sent off to *HMS King Alfred* in Hove, Thomas completed the ten-week course with flying colours, and was then attached to a newly-commissioned flower-class corvette. He joined this ship, as captain, in the Harland and Wolff yard where it had been built. Nursed by fussy tugs, the *Amarylis* slipped out into Belfast Lough, the sound of its exultant siren echoing back from the Black Mountain that broods above the city. Sea trials lay ahead, a busy week of criss-crossing between the coasts of

Northern Ireland and Ayrshire, ironing out any lurking faults in the machinery on which, in a short space of time, their lives, and the lives of all those they escorted, might depend.

The Sound of Mull

It all seemed slightly unreal to him. The air-raids that people had spoken of had not materialised; shipping moved about largely unmolested; French and British armies were entrenched in Europe and would surely deter any further German adventurism; the Maginot Line bristled with armaments; the shops were full enough with the necessities of life – no western skies, it seemed, had fallen. And yet the depth charges that were loaded on the ship were real enough; the ammunition stored in the magazines was not blank; and at some time, he knew, there would be a reckoning.

Now he was sent to the Sound of Mull for training in the art of tracking a submarine. The sound of the ship's sonar detector, the sharp, echoing *ping*, became an extra heart-beat – constant, reassuring, the vital point of the entire ship and its crew. All that human effort, all that disruption of lives, was focused in that thin sliver of sound. That was the reason why they were there – to send that probing signal down into the depths, day in, day out. And then, of course, to unleash explosive force against the men and machinery detected beneath them. This was what war ultimately came to. First there were the words, the rhetoric, the posturing; then came the brutal business of trying to shoot or drown those on the other side.

The Captain thought hard about that. It was not in his nature to wish harm on anybody. He was gentle in his disposition. That was what Mr J.M.C. Robinson had spotted all those years ago: he had sensed that the Captain had the capacity to *understand*. And now that capacity meant that he saw only too clearly the cruelty and ambition of the dictators, and the hatred they proclaimed. And that made this the moment for other things to be put aside. It was not a time for selfishness; it was, rather, a time of sacrifice and for doing what was asked of one. The Captain never questioned that, not once. Ships would go down – he knew that – and his might be one. But that was not something one would wish to dwell upon, and he did not. He immersed himself in the work of the moment, as people were doing, uncomplainingly, up and down the country. He listened to the sonar. It was hypnotic. He felt the ship beneath him, its engines, its power, its vulnerability. Mr J.M.C. Robinson came to mind, that gentle pedagogue, and he imagined what he might say. *Your ship is a metaphor.* Yes, but so were U-boats, and the Atlantic swell, and the cold water that stretched all the way over to Canada and America and that was merciless in its dealings with men and the ships in which they sailed.

Tobermory Harbour

The Captain had worked out the odds of survival and thought that, on balance, it was unlikely that he would see out more than two years of convoy duty. In fact, he had lasted slightly longer than that by the time he was promoted and sent to a shore posting in Tobermory, on the Isle of Mull. Even so, he asked to remain at sea, but his request was turned down. Experienced sailors were needed for training positions, and he fitted the bill perfectly. And so it was that the Captain spent the reminder of the war living in a large stone house, a former manse, overlooking the busy harbour of Tobermory. He shared with more junior officers attending courses, and a succession of Polish naval commanders who found themselves exiled in Scotland. It was not ideal, but it was better than the lot that many of their countrymen were experiencing. The Captain wrote a poem that he called *The Country Within Us*. The Poles listened gravely while one, whose English was rather better, translated for the other. One of them wept. "He is weeping not just for your words," his friend said, "but for everything. For our country, Poland. For our families. For the world." The Captain gave the weeping man the piece of paper on which he had written out the poem. The man folded it carefully and tucked it into a pocket of his tunic. He said something in Polish, which the other man translated as, "He says that he will keep this close to his heart." Then he said, "He also says that you are his brother."

During the first two years of the war, He and Elsie saw one another when their leaves coincided, which was not often. She was stationed then in Glasgow, where she was a nursing auxiliary at the Victoria Infirmary. In 1942 she was posted to Cairo, from where, in due course, she was moved to Sicily following the landing of the 51st Highland Division in 1943. They wrote to one another, although it took a long time for her letters to arrive from the theatre of operations in Italy. Her letters changed in tone, he thought, as the war progressed. At first they had been easy in their intimacy; now they seemed more formal, more distant, as if they were being written out of duty. He said in a letter, "You don't have to write to me every week, you know. The occasional word is nice – just to let me know that all is well – but please don't think it's a duty."

She wrote back, "Don't you want to hear about what's happening to me? I suppose I should understand that. We haven't seen one another for so long and it's easy to forget what the other person is like. I still think of you, you know, but it seems to me that you're somehow fading away in my mind – like a picture that's losing its definition. I don't know if I should even be telling you that, but that's what's happening. This war has taught me to be honest, I suppose – even to the point of heartlessness – or so it seems."

It was three weeks before he replied, and a further month before she received his letter. He said, "Dearest Elsie, I don't know what's happening between us. The last thing I want you to feel is that you are bound to me in some way – and by that I mean bound by something other than affection or love, or whatever you want to call it. I think that we have both become different people from those we were when we both went off at the beginning of this whole wretched business. That happens, I think. Indeed, it would be odd if it didn't. It would be odd if none of us were changed by the things we do and see in these unusual times. If you think that you are so different now that it would be hard for us to be with one another again, then I shall understand. And you mustn't feel guilty about it. I have no time for those who try to make others feel guilty just because they are being human."

He was not sure what response he would get to that letter, but even so he was surprised when her answer came back a couple of months later. "Dear Thomas, I wouldn't be telling you this if I thought you wouldn't understand. I would never want to hurt you, but I know that you prefer to know the truth about things. I have met somebody else now and try as I might I have not been able to stop myself falling in love with him. I really did make an effort to keep myself from doing this, but it was too much for me. I could try to blame the war. I could say it's all the fault of what is happening about us, but I don't think I should do that. It's my fault. I have allowed it to happen, and once you let something like this get a foot in the door, you can't do much about it. Do I still love you? Yes, I do. But I love Geoffrey too, and I have had to decide between the two of you. I have chosen him – not because he is any better than you, but because he is here – he works in the hospital with me; he is a surgeon – and you are there and when you think you could die any day you reach out for whatever happiness you can get."

He lowered the letter. He looked out over the Sound of Mull. He closed his eyes briefly and then opened them again. He thought that he might cry – it seemed like that to him – but he did not; it was as if the war had exhausted his supply of tears. He felt quite calm, as people say they do even as disaster embraces them. You watch it reveal itself, slowly, and you feel quite calm, as if what is happening is happening not to you but to somebody else.

He picked up the letter once more. There was a final page that he now read, although the paper was shaking in his hands. A few lines on a page could so easily end a world.

"I want to give you something, as I feel that we have shared everything equally right from the start. I would like to keep the hotel because that has always been in the family and it means a lot to me. I may not be there to run it, but I have Mr Duncan, and he knows exactly what he's doing. I shall make him a partner in the business when the war is over."

"But you will remember that I have that old place up in Morvern, that I got from my McGibbon aunts, that old chapel that nobody wanted and that you always said could be put to good use. You'll remember that there are about twenty acres attached to it and you also said that something could be done with those too – a croft, perhaps. I'd like you to have that. You could keep a boat up there and farm a bit and I think you could be happy. You might meet somebody – who knows? I have written to Mr Maclean, who is one of the solicitors in Fort William. He says he can arrange everything. This is what I want to do. I want you to accept this, not only because you deserve it, but because it will make me feel less guilty about what has happened. Please don't

The old chapel that nobody wanted

argue about it. Please accept it as being the thing that I really want to do."

His first thought was that he would ignore this offer. He wanted nothing from her; he had his pride. But then he thought that it would be churlish to refuse this gift and, anyway, his refusal would make her feel worse. He did not want that. He had no desire to harm her because there was so much unhappiness as it was, with this wretched war, and everybody was quite miserable enough as it was. So he wrote back and told her that he was sorry that this had happened but that he understood. It was very kind of her to give him the old chapel and he would try to fix it up after the war. "It has that great view over towards Tobermory," he wrote. "I may even live there myself."

The outcome of the war was now obvious, but the Captain still found himself surprised by the cessation of hostilities. It seemed such an anti-climax after years of struggle and he was not at all sure of what he would do with his time. His years in the Navy had been a time during which the major decisions of his life had been taken for him by his superiors and by the rule book he followed. Now the shape of his future was in his own hands, and he was not sure what to do with the unfamiliar freedom.

He had his reservations about returning to Oban; it had always been Elsie's world rather than his. But when he learned that she was going to Australia with her new husband, he overcame his reluctance to go back to the town in which they had both lived. She had sold the hotel before she left for Melbourne, and the new owners had changed its name. The man with whom he had shared the fishing boat was eager to resume their partnership, and the Captain agreed, mainly because he had no other idea of what to do. They took on a boy called Eric, and they trained him in the ways of fishermen. He walked with a slight limp – the result of an unexplained accident – and had dark hair that fell down over his brow, obscuring his eyes. He spoke Gaelic and wanted to go to America. He never did. After working on the trawler for six years he went off one weekend to see a football match in Glasgow and never returned. He had met a butcher's daughter in a pub, and had married her a few weeks later. His new father-in-law took him on in the butchery, that was expanding at the time. That expansion continued and eventually the business became a string of fourteen butcheries, making a wealthy man of the young fisherman from Oban.

The Captain spent much of his spare time on restoring the classic yacht he had bought before the war. He was a skilled carpenter, and one by one the boat's timbers were replaced by lovingly crafted substitutes. It was not long before the boat came to be considered one of the most beautiful vessels on the west coast of Scotland. The Captain began to use it to take visitors up to Skye and, on occasion, out to St Kilda. As word got round of this graceful yacht, he found himself spending more and more time on these charters, at the expense of his fishing. Eventually, he sold his share in the trawler and settled down to the life of a professional yachtsman, making himself available for charter.

It is not widely known that Ernest Hemingway visited Scotland on two occasions in the late nineteen-fifties. None of Hemingway's biographers mention these visits, nor do they record the correspondence between the Captain and the writer. On both of his trips to Scotland, Hemingway spent almost all his time in Oban and Tobermory, embarking from both of these harbours for voyages up to the Small Isles and Skye. The Captain was able to introduce Hemingway to Gavin Maxwell, the naturalist whose domesticated otters had so entertained the world with their exploits. When they met, Maxwell's *Ring of Bright Water* was yet to be published, and Maxwell was still living in his lonely cottage looking out towards Skye and the Cuillins. The Captain spent more than one convivial evening with Maxwell at Sandaig, drinking whisky beside a peat fire while Hemingway regaled his small audience with tales of fishing off Key West.

It was possibly under the influence of these two friends – Maxwell and Hemingway – that the Captain began to explore a suggestion made many years previously by Mr J.M.C. Robinson, that he should try his hand at writing poetry. "I think you might be able to do it," the English teacher had said. "Sometimes poetry is just below the surface, you know, and all it takes is a nudge to bring it into existence."

The Captain wrote a sonnet while sailing back from Skye with Hemingway. He showed it to his friend. "This is very good," Hemingway said. Encouraged by this praise from a master, the Captain began to produce regular short poems on maritime and insular subjects. A few years later a collection, *Of the Sea and of Islands*, was published by the Glasgow publisher, William MacLellan, in his *Poetry Scotland* series. The cover of this book was designed by William Crosbie, a Scottish artist who had studied in Paris under Braque. *Of the Sea and of Islands* was well received but little mention was made of it after the last of its six hundred copies was sold. Although other volumes in the *Poetry Scotland* series turn up from time to time on the shelves of second-hand booksellers, the Captain's book is rarely seen today. Five of the sonnets, along with a poem in a different metre, *The Sea Between Us*, are reproduced at the end of this memoir.

The Captain had told Elsie that he might take up residence in the old chapel on the Drimnin Road, and this he did in the spring of 1955. At first he lived in the chapel itself, but after a few months he decided that the view from the site would be greatly improved if he were to build on top of the building's flat roof. Employing his skills as a carpenter, he constructed an oval-shaped cabin on top of the roof, from the front of which he could look out directly towards Tobermory. This cabin had a sitting room that doubled up as a study, a bedroom, a small kitchen, and a rudimentary bathroom. It was perfect for the Captain's bachelor existence.

The Captain acquired a dog named Alastair Macpherson. This was rather a formal name for a dog, most dogs being denied a surname. In Alastair's case, though, the name seemed quite in keeping with his reputation, which was considerable. Alastair Macpherson was a sheep dog, with all the intelligence of his breed. He was a good companion, and yet the Captain was lonely. During the war there had been a great deal of company, and he missed that in his remote corner of Morvern. He was a shy man, though, and he was worried that women would not be interested in him. Eventually plucking up his courage, he wrote to an introduction agency he had seen advertised in the *Glasgow Herald*. He was interested in meeting a suitable lady, he said, and could they please enrol him on their books with a view to arranging an introduction.

It was through the *Clyde Romances* agency that he met Moira, a singing teacher from Helensburgh. They both sensed almost immediately that they were perfectly suited to one another, and they married three months later in Lochgilphead, where they both had friends and knew the Church of Scotland minister.

It was a blissfully happy marriage. Moira made a comfortable home for them in the old chapel, while leaving the cabin to the Captain for his memorabilia of the sea. They lived there until 1979, when the Captain caught pneumonia, was taken to Inverness for treatment, and died two days later. Moira moved back to live with a sister in Helensburgh, where she ran a boarding house for a few years before her death in 1983.

The old chapel was sold. The Captain's cabin was dismantled by the new owners and the wood used to make a large hen house in the back garden. The Captain's possessions, his sextant, his pictures, his chairs from the *Arcadia*, were given to Ardtornish Estate to use in the furnishing of one of the estate cottages. The

Captain's yacht returned to the Clyde, where it was briefly the flagship of the Commodore of the Royal Northern Yacht Club.

Saloon chairs from Arcadia in the Captain's Cabin

Do buildings have a spirit – an essence that lingers in the place where they once stood, and that may emerge if somebody chooses to recreate what stood there before? It is perhaps true that there linger in place vague echoes, resonances perhaps, of what was once there. Although nothing remained of the cabin constructed on the roof of the old chapel, people who looked at the building often expressed the view that there must have been something there before, and that whatever it was had left some *feeling* behind. Locals remembered, of course, that there had been a cabin, and they could have told visitors about it, but what was significant was that those who came completely afresh to the site, with no knowledge of how it had looked before, should somehow sense the presence of something. "One day," one visitor remarked, "somebody will build something up there – to take advantage of the view over towards Mull."

The Captain had never been a particularly wealthy man, but because of judicious investments, when he died his estate was worth several hundred thousand pounds. It was left entirely to Moira, but in a precatory bequest he asked her that she should use any surplus to help young people from cities who might benefit from a few weeks in the country. This was a cause on which the

Captain had often expressed views. He felt that a spell on a farm, possibly coupled with a few days at sea, could turn around a life that was going wrong in the cramped conditions of a big city. Moira agreed with him on this, and since she had a small income of her own – sufficient, though, for her needs while living with her sister – she began to use the Captain's inheritance to sponsor such breaks for children from the Gorbals. In this work she was helped and advised by a young minister who had been influenced by the legendary Scottish churchman, George Macleod, founder of the Iona Community and a passionate advocate of social justice and the healing power of love and compassion. George Macleod came from a long line of Church of Scotland ministers who had lived at Fiunary House, not far from the Captain's cabin. He saw how young lives could be changed in this way, and had inspired this young minister to identify boys whose lives were stunted by poverty, cruelty and indifference. They were taken off for a period of a few weeks to farms in Argyll and sometimes further afield, where they were boarded with the families of shepherds and cattlemen. They helped to bring in the harvest, to stack peats, and to bring sheep in to the flank. They soon forgot about the gangs and hard culture of the streets. "It works," said the minister. "I have seen it with my own eyes. It works."

Some thirty-five years after the Captain's death, the old chapel changed hands again. Now it was acquired by Roderick James, an architect known for his imagination and who had already designed several beguiling buildings at that end of the Morvern peninsula. Roderick had seen pictures of the Captain's Cabin, shown him by Hugh Raven, and decided that he would recreate it, this time using more permanent materials. Wood, however well-preserved, can suffer from the extreme weather of those parts, and Roderick opted to use metal. The lay-out, though, was exactly that which the Captain had chosen, and he was able to retrieve from Hugh Raven's care many of the items that had furnished the cabin in the Captain's day. Once again, the photographs of boats were on the walls, the models of ships on shelves, and the chairs retrieved from his father's vessel placed where they had been in the past, affording the same view over the quiet waters of the Sound of Mull.

The Saloon in the Captain's Cabin

Few people still remembered the Captain although a number of older people could be traced who had some recollections of him. Their memories of him were fond ones. The Captain had had no enemies. He kept he own counsel. He shared what he had.

One man, a retired ferry captain, made particular mention of the Captain's dog, Alastair Macpherson. "There was a very strange thing about that dog," he said. "He had second sight, you know. You come across people from time to time who have second sight – it's a big thing in the Highlands – but you don't expect to find it in a dog. Yet he had it.'

The Captain's dog, Alastair Macpherson

He gave several examples. "When the Captain was off at sea, Alastair Macpherson would wait down near the pier. He knew, though, when the Captain left Oban to return, round the point of Lismore, for the final stage of the journey back to Lochaline. There was no possibility of his seeing the yacht – it was all this special sense that he had."

"He could also predict storms. If snow was on its way, he would whimper, well before there was the slightest indication in the sky, or in the wind, of the weather turning. And, most striking of all, was his capacity to predict the prospect of a marriage. If a couple were well-matched, he would wait outside the church and chase his tail with delight when they emerged newly married. If he sensed that the marriage was ill-starred, he would sit morosely at the side of the kirk, his head lowered in foreboding. It was quite extraordinary, and not what one expected to find in a sheep dog."

"And another thing, he was a Gaelic-speaking dog. He refused to obey any order in English and would wait until the same instruction was given in Gaelic before he complied. This was a mystery to the Captain, who had only a few words of Gaelic, and who had owned the dog from puppyhood. How can a dog know Gaelic if he has not been brought up in a Gaelic-speaking household? Can you explain that to me?"

Roderick listened to all of this in astonishment. He did not exactly disbelieve what he heard, but then again he did not quite believe it. Sometimes there are things that we want to believe in, but find it difficult, and feel an understandable regret that colourful details should not be true.

Bedroom at the Captain's Cabin

This is more or less all that I managed to learn about the Captain and the Captain's father. The picture that emerged was not one that required a wide canvas: I came to see it as more of a miniature, completed with gentle strokes, of two lives that were very much lives of their time, but that were, for all that, out of the ordinary, and were so in a good way. There is a coda, though, to the story, and this coda demonstrates, perhaps, that there attaches, to the lives of all us, a penumbra of effect – the legacy, the aftertaste, so to speak, of the few years that we pass on this earth, that earth that the poet, Norman McCaig, described as "this poor, sad bearer of wars and disasters". That legacy is found in the continued effect of things we might have done – lives that were changed, one hopes for the better, by some minor achievement, some small amelioration of the travails of those amongst whom we live. Shortly after the renewed Captain's cabin had arisen where the earlier one had been, a farmer from Wiltshire, Jamie Feilden, happened to visit Morvern. Roderick James showed him the cabin and they stood for a while looking out over the Sound of Mull. Roderick gave Jamie the broad outlines of the Captain's story, and told him of the way in which the Captain had given troubled youths a chance to turn their lives around. Jamie listened carefully. Then he said, "But that is what we do too." And he explained how his farms had opened their doors to children who needed a fresh start, who needed somebody to believe in them, needed somebody to love them. "Perhaps we can have Captain's cabins on the farms I use for this," he said.

"You could," said Roderick.

And so a life that was not, on the face of things, so very unusual or successful, continued to touch the lives of those for whom the world had been a difficult or a trying place; made those lives a bit better, and in this way made the world more the place that all of us would wish it to be.

Cabin & Sundeck

APPENDIX:

EXCERPTS FROM *Of the Sea and of Islands*

The Captain's Sonnets of Sea and Islands

Taking a view

The sea, when quiet, can make a sailor feel
A glassy surface and unruffled calm
Could not involve the slightest risk of harm;
Nor danger here will wavelets dare conceal;
The tide shifts gently in the bay,
The glass will hold, no sudden rise nor fall,
Pressure high, no warning word at all
Is necessary; fair stands the wind, they say.
How wrong the optimist in his forecast,
We prefer the cautious old sea-dog
Who enters in his vessel's daily log
The sage remark: fair weather cannot last.

Always assume the worst and then be glad
When conditions, it transpires, are not so bad.

Charts and the inner self

A chart, if read correctly, is there to help
To keep the average vessel off the shore,
And on occasion may even tell us more
Of what lies below, of sand and rock and kelp,

All things a careful sailor should avoid,
Just as, in life, our inner map explains
The burdens, guilts, and all the psychic strains
That were revealed to us by Sigmund Freud.
Of all, he knew, just how hard we try
To be ourselves, while one thing and another
Is done to us, unwittingly, by mother:
And orchestrates this truth: few men can cry.

All men who go to sea find out at last:
There is no tide that can wipe out your past.

Ships' Cooks

A good ship's cook is rather hard to find,
They have a temper, swear, and cut up rough,
Are taciturn misanthropes – and tough;
Some captains smile, and say they do not mind,
But that's not me: I much prefer to know
Who crews my ship, his provenance, I'd say,
Needs scrutiny before we sail away;
Always be aware, I warn, of just who's down below.
One chef we had, his cooking was the tops,
He could transform a herring, make a stew,
There was nothing much we found he couldn't do;
Then we discovered he was wanted by the cops.

At sea you'd best avoid the fancy dish,
Enjoy your hard-tack biscuits and your pickled fish!

SS Arcadia

How to choose a good ship

A passage on the sea is East to West,
Or North to South, it all depends
On where the distant owner comes to send
His vessel, and which route seems best
For current weather, and for tides,
For needs of commerce, and the cargo
Taken on; ship-brokers, to a man, will show
The soundest ship, and such things besides
As will make a merchant understand
His goods are safe, he need not fret
About demurrage, and that yet
His orders will be met, are all in hand.

Never choose a ship because she's fast:
Look at the men who stand before her mast.

The things of childhood

I often think how it is as boys
We are so proud to have in our possession
Little signs of passion or obsession,
A favourite penknife, other toys
That mean a lot, model soldiers,
Made of lead and painted fine by hand
In regimental colours, a whole band
Of tiny, brightly tartaned pipers,
These I cherished, but can't forget
A full-rigged ship my father gave to me
A tiny ship upon a tiny sea,
I loved it so, and will admit I love it yet.

A little ship took me off to sea,
My father's gift has meant the world to me.

Excerpt from *The Sea Between Us*, a longer poem written by
the Captain in 1962. This poem was written for a friend, David
MacDonald, whom he came to know in Tobermory during the
War. David was a doctor, who later went to Rwanda to run a
mission hospital. The Captain never saw him again after that. He
described David as the best friend he had ever had.

Mission Hospital at Shyira, Rwanda

Dear friend, since you went away
I've written twice, failed to post the letter,
Fearing you might not find the time
To bother with my thoughts;
Friendship is something that is hard to paint
In words, in ink, on something so insubstantial
As a piece of writing paper; an orchestra,
Complete with chorus, is what friendship deserves,
But very rarely gets; love requires that too,
Although I have never quite understood
The distinction between the two,
Perhaps I shall on that dreadful day
When we say a real goodbye,
And I shall cry buckets, as I know I shall,
In my ordinary conviction that we always
Had something particular to say to one another;
Seas between us move, that island we both knew,
Is green still; Ben More still surveys
The places we walked in that emergency;
The boat I would send for you, if ever I do,
Will be frail, will be delicate;
Wait for it by the shore, do not let it pass.

JAMIE'S FARM.
Cultivating Change.

Jamie's Farm aims to act as a catalyst for change; enabling disadvantaged young people, at risk of social and academic exclusion, to be better equipped to thrive academically, socially and emotionally during their school years and beyond.

Mealtime at Jamie's Farm

We do this primarily through a unique residential experience and follow-up programme involving 'Farming, Family, Therapy and Legacy'. During the week up to 12 young people, accompanied by two to three members of staff from their school/ organisation, are involved with the running of one of our four rural working livestock farms in Bath, Hereford, Monmouth and Lewes. Visiting young people complete real jobs with tangible outcomes. Activities include farming, gardening, cooking, horse work, log chopping, music and crafts, as well as a daily walk in the countryside. Alongside this, we provide one-to-one and group reflective sessions to support young people to vocalise rather than act out their challenges and develop new positive behaviour patterns to carry forward into home and school life. Their visit is followed by a rigorous follow-up programme aimed at ensuring positive changes are sustained. We also run Oasis Farm Waterloo, where we deliver follow-up, and longer-term, programmes for our London partners.

Cattle at Jamie's Farm

Everyday farming tasks

We also aim to achieve our vision through spreading our approach and enabling systemic change, by profoundly influencing the way the education system works, training teachers and other professionals in multiple sectors to engage more effectively with disadvantaged young people, as well as informing and supporting parents and society at large to enable all young people to thrive.